The Alpha Sheriff

A Protective Alpha Sheriff Fated Mates Omegaverse Romance

Ash Jade

Dear Reader,

Welcome to Sanctuary, a hidden mountain town whispered about in the wider omegaverse, a place where worn-down omegas come to heal and alphas learn that strength is measured in gentleness, not dominance. If you've made it this far, maybe part of you is curious... or hopeful... or simply ready to step into a world where instinct doesn't have to hurt, and where every story bends toward safety, connection, and a well-earned happily-ever-after.

Here, the omegaverse works a little differently.

Alphas, betas, and omegas still move through life guided by pheromones, instincts, and bonds, but Sanctuary is a refuge, one carved out of grief, rebuilt with stubborn hope, and held together by a pack that refuses to let anyone fall through the cracks. Heats and ruts still come like wild weather, but they're met with care, consent, and hands that steady instead of seize. And sometimes, the mountain air carries something more ancient still: the pull of fated mates, that quiet click inside your chest when you realize home might be a person as much as a place.

Each novella in this series is a fast, high-heat, heart-forward escape. A story about a protective alpha, a brave omega, and the slow re-teaching of trust. You can read them in order or wander in wherever you like. Every couple stands alone, yet each book threads another stitch into the found-family tapestry of Sanctuary.

Before you step inside, a few gentle warnings:

These stories contain explicit sexual content, primal dynamics, instinct-driven tension, and adult themes. They are not dark romance, but they *do* explore trauma recovery, vulnerability, and the process of learning to choose yourself again. Please honor your comfort level and step away if something doesn't sit right with you.

Additional content considerations: violence, injury, death, mentions of sexual violence (not depicted but discussed), and themes of healing from past harm.

If Sanctuary sounds like somewhere you might want to linger—if you're ready for protective alphas, fierce omegas, small-town gossip, soft pack dinners, and bonds that bloom where hurt once lived—then settle in.

The mountains are waiting.
— Ash Jade

CONTENTS

1

I grip Emma's small hand tighter as we step off the bus, the last dregs of our money spent getting to this nowhere town called Sanctuary. Fitting name, if it delivers on the promise. My daughter's tired eyes peer up at me, trust and exhaustion warring in them, and I force a smile I don't feel. Five years old and she's already spent half her life running. The air here smells different—pine, dirt, and something indefinably pure. No trace of alpha pheromones marking territory, at least not immediately. Maybe we actually found it this time. A place to disappear.

"Mommy, my feet hurt," Emma whines, tugging at my hand.

"I know, baby. Just a little further." I hoist our single duffel higher on my shoulder. Everything we own, stuffed into one pathetic bag. I'm too tired to feel the shame anymore.

Sanctuary is smaller than I expected—a main street with faded storefronts, a diner with neon that flickers even in daylight, and a squat brick building that must be the sheriff's office. People move unhurriedly, stopping to chat on corners. Small town life. I'd forgotten what it looked like.

"Is this home now?" Emma asks, her voice small but hopeful.

The question cuts deeper than she knows. "We'll see. First, we need a place to sleep."

The motel stands at the edge of town—a single-story stretch of rooms with peeling blue paint and a blinking vacancy sign. Better than sleeping in a bus station again. The office door jingles as I push it open, Emma half-hiding behind my legs.

The beta behind the counter looks up from her magazine, eyes narrowing slightly as she scents us. Omega and pup, no alpha. Her judgment hangs in the air between us.

"Need a room," I say, not bothering with pleasantries. "Cheapest you've got."

She snaps her gum. "Fifty a night. Weekly rate's two-fifty."

I dig into my pocket, fingers trembling slightly as I count out bills. Three hundred left after the room. Maybe enough for food for two weeks if I'm careful. Then what?

"How long you staying?" she asks, sliding a key across the counter.

"Not sure yet." The standard non-answer of someone who doesn't want to be found.

Her eyes flick to Emma, then back to me. A flicker of something—pity?—crosses her face. "Room 7. End of the row. Quietest spot." She hesitates. "Diner's hiring. Case you're looking."

I nod, surprised by the kindness. "Thanks."

Emma tugs at my jacket as we leave the office. "I'm hungry, Mommy."

"Soon, baby." I unlock our room—musty, dated, but clean enough. Two beds with faded floral spreads. A TV that probably gets three channels. Bathroom with a tub that might actually hold water. "Why don't you pick your bed while I get our things sorted?"

While Emma bounces experimentally between beds, I unpack our meager belongings. Clean clothes in the dresser. Toothbrushes in the bathroom. Emma's stuffed wolf—the one thing I made sure she kept through everything—placed carefully on her chosen bed. Routine in chaos. The pretense of normalcy.

I'm hanging my two shirts in the closet when it hits me—a scent cutting through the stale motel air. Alpha. Strong, clean, like pine and smoke and something primal that makes my omega hindbrain sit up and take notice. My hands freeze mid-motion.

"Emma, stay inside," I say, trying to keep my voice steady. "Mommy needs to check something."

I crack the door, peering out cautiously. Across the street, a man stands beside a sheriff's cruiser, his attention fixed directly on our motel room. Tall, broad-shouldered, with dark hair and the unmistakable stance of an alpha in his prime. The sheriff's badge on his chest catches sunlight.

My heart slams against my ribs. How? We've been here less than an hour. Has Marcus already tracked us? Did he call ahead?

But no—this doesn't feel like danger. The alpha across the street isn't moving toward us, isn't showing aggression. He's just... watching. And something else is happening. A pull. A recognition that buzzes beneath my skin like electricity.

Our eyes lock across the distance, and the world narrows to a pinpoint.

Mate.

The word surfaces from some primal part of my brain, and I slam the door shut before the thought can fully form. No. Impossible. Dangerous thinking. I don't have a true mate—I have a psychotic ex and a daughter to protect.

"Mommy?" Emma stands in the middle of the room, her small face creased with worry. "Is the bad man here?"

I force my breathing to slow, crouching to her level. "No, baby. No bad men. Just checking." I brush her dark curls back from her forehead.

"Are you still hungry? Let's get some food in that tummy."

She nods, instantly distracted by the promise of food, but I can't shake the feeling that clings to me. That scent. That pull. The weight of the sheriff's gaze.

I peek through the curtains. He's still there, though he's turned slightly away now, speaking into a radio. His profile is strong, jaw set in a hard line. Not at all like Marcus, whose handsome face always hid the cruelty beneath. This alpha seems... solid. Steady.

Dangerous thoughts, Olivia.

I let the curtain fall, scooping Emma into my arms despite her protests that she's "a big girl now."

"We're going to be okay here," I whisper, more to myself than to her. "We just need to be careful. Very careful."

But as I hold my daughter, that unfamiliar scent still lingers in my nostrils, and something long dormant stirs in my chest that I choose not to examine too closely.

2

By morning, I've convinced myself yesterday's reaction was stress and exhaustion. Mate pull? Please. That's fairy tale stuff for omegas who've never had an alpha's hand around their throat. I focus on practical things—getting Emma fed, finding the cheapest place to buy groceries, scouting the town's exits. But when the sheriff's cruiser rolls past the motel for the third time before noon, my body betrays me. Heart racing, palms damp, scent glands warming at my neck. Ridiculous. Dangerous. I duck back inside our room, ignoring Emma's questions.

"Can I play outside, Mommy? Please?" Emma bounces on the bed, too much energy trapped in her small body after yesterday's long journey.

"Not right now, baby." I peer through the curtains again. The cruiser is gone, but that doesn't mean he isn't watching. "How about we color instead?"

She pouts but accepts the worn coloring book and broken crayons I fish from our bag. As she scribbles, I make mental calculations. We can't stay locked in this room forever. I need to find work. Emma needs fresh air, school eventually. We can't keep running.

Maybe he's just doing his job. Small-town sheriff, new faces in town. Doesn't mean he knows about Marcus. Doesn't mean anything.

"Your picture's all messy, Mommy." Emma frowns at my distracted scribbles.

"Sorry, sweetheart." I force a smile. "Let's get some lunch, then maybe we can explore a little."

The diner across from the motel serves greasy burgers that Emma devours while I pick at fries, scanning faces, exits, threats. No one pays us special attention. No cruisers pass by.

"Can I play now?" Emma asks as we return to the motel, her eyes on the small patch of grass with a single bench near our room.

The rational part of me says no. The part that sees her pale face, her need for normalcy, says yes.

"Just right here where I can see you." I settle on the bench with our motel room door open behind me. "Don't go anywhere else, okay?"

"Promise!" She skips off to examine a patch of dandelions.

I keep my eyes on her while mentally planning our next steps. The diner is hiring. I could start tomorrow if they'll take me. Maybe find a small apartment after a few paychecks. Enroll Emma in kindergarten. Pretend we're normal.

A woman approaches from the motel office, calling something about clean towels. I turn to answer her, just for a moment.

When I look back, Emma is gone.

"Emma?" The dandelions sway empty in the breeze. "Emma!"

I'm on my feet, panic clawing up my throat. Not again. Not here.

"EMMA!" I scan the parking lot, the road, the spaces between buildings.

"She was just—" The motel woman starts.

I don't wait for her to finish. I'm running, calling Emma's name, my heart a hammer against my ribs. Marcus couldn't have found us already. He couldn't. But what if—

I round the corner of the motel and freeze.

The sheriff—the alpha from yesterday—is crouched at eye level with Emma, his large frame somehow made non-threatening as he speaks softly to my daughter. Emma is nodding, clutching her stuffed wolf to her chest.

Terror and relief collide in my chest.

"Emma!" My voice comes out sharper than intended.

She turns, face brightening. "Mommy! I found a cat but it runned away!"

I rush forward, dropping to my knees to pull her against me, inhaling her scent to confirm she's safe, unharmed. My fingers tremble as I check her over.

"I told you not to wander off," I say, voice tight with leftover fear. "You promised."

"I'm sorry," she whispers, lower lip wobbling. "The kitty was orange."

Only then do I allow myself to look up at the sheriff. This close, his scent is overwhelming—pine and clean sweat and alpha strength. My omega responds with a rush of warmth I ruthlessly suppress.

"She was headed for the street," he says, his voice deep but gentle. "Chasing a stray cat."

"Thank you." The words feel inadequate. "I just—I looked away for a second."

"Kids are quick." He smiles, and something inside me twists. It's a good smile—not predatory, not calculating. It reaches his eyes, crinkling the corners. "I'm Jake Hawkins. Sheriff."

"Olivia," I offer, not giving our last name. "This is Emma."

"Are you the police?" Emma asks, suddenly forgetting her tears. "Do you have a gun?"

"Emma!" I hiss, mortified.

Jake laughs, the sound warm and genuine. "I am the police. And yes, I have a gun, but I only use it to protect people."

Emma nods solemnly. "Like from bad guys."

Something passes across his face—a flicker of assessment. "That's right. From bad guys."

I stand, pulling Emma with me. "We should get back to our room."

"Of course." He rises too, and I'm acutely aware of his height, the breadth of his shoulders. Not threatening, but solid. Present. "Are you folks staying in town long?"

The question sounds casual, but I catch the careful way he watches me. He's good—better than most alphas at hiding his interest. But I've learned to read the signs.

"Not sure yet," I answer, the same non-answer I gave the motel clerk.

He nods, respecting the evasion. "Well, if you need anything—directions, recommendations, help of any kind—the station's just down Main Street. Or you can ask for me here." He hands me a card. "My cell's on there too."

Our fingers brush as I take it, and the jolt is immediate, electric. His pupils dilate slightly, confirming he felt it too.

"The diner's good for breakfast," he offers, stepping back slightly. "And they're hiring, if you're looking for work."

"So I've heard." I tuck the card into my pocket without looking at it. "Thank you again. For finding her."

"Anytime." His eyes linger on mine a moment longer than necessary. "Take care, Olivia. Emma."

He tips his hat to Emma, who giggles and waves, then walks back toward his cruiser.

I watch him go, the card burning a hole in my pocket. My neck tingles where my scent glands have warmed, responding to his proximity. It would be so easy to call him back, to ask for help, to lean on his obvious strength.

And that's exactly why I can't.

"I like the police man," Emma announces as I lead her back to our room. "He smells nice."

Out of the mouths of babes. I squeeze her hand, not trusting my voice.

Nice isn't what we need. Safe is what we need. And I learned the hard way that alphas are never safe—no matter how good they smell or how kind their smiles.

But as I close our motel room door, I can't help bringing my fingers to my nose, catching the lingering trace of his scent where our hands touched. Pine and protection and possibility.

I'm in trouble.

3

I wake at 3 AM with my skin on fire. At first, I think it's a fever—then the familiar ache blooms low in my belly, and I know. Heat. Three months early and completely unexpected. I curl into a ball, biting my pillow to stifle a groan. This can't be happening. Not here. Not now. I haven't had a natural heat in years—suppressants have kept me clinical, controlled, invisible to alphas. But the stress of running, the abrupt change in environment, the sudden feeling of safety—my treacherous omega biology has decided now is the perfect time to announce my fertility to every alpha within miles.

"Mommy?" Emma's sleepy voice comes from the other bed. "Are you sick?"

"Just a little, baby." I force my voice to sound normal. "Go back to sleep."

She mumbles something and rolls over, clutching her wolf. Thank god she's too young to understand what's happening.

I drag myself to the bathroom, legs already shaky, and splash cold water on my face. My reflection is a nightmare—flushed cheeks, dilated pupils, a thin sheen of sweat making my skin glow. I can smell myself—honey and spice and unmistakable fertility. The scent will seep through doors, windows, vents. It's already filling our small room.

Think, Olivia.

I rummage through our bag, hoping for forgotten suppressants, but find nothing. The pharmacy won't open for hours, and I don't have a prescription anyway. We need to leave, find somewhere isolated, but I can barely stand without my knees trembling. Driving is out of the question.

By 4 AM, I've soaked through my shirt. The cramps intensify, waves of need making me press my thighs together. I've barricaded the door with the room's single chair, but it's a joke. Any determined alpha could break it down with one kick.

Emma sleeps on, oblivious. I watch her innocent face and feel sick with fear. I've spent years protecting her from Marcus, from his pack, from the ugly reality of what her mother is—an omega whose biology makes her vulnerable to any alpha who decides to claim her. And now here I am, sending out a biological flare that says "come and get it" to every alpha in Sanctuary.

At 5 AM, I hear them. Car doors slamming too close to our room. Low voices, masculine laughter. Footsteps circling the building. I peek through the curtains and see them—three men in the parking lot, heads raised, scenting the air. Strangers, not Marcus's pack, but dangerous all the same. Heat-drunk alphas don't ask permission.

"Emma." I shake her gently. "Emma, wake up."

She blinks sleepily. "Is it morning?"

"We need to go somewhere else." I help her sit up, trying to keep my hands steady. "Can you help Mommy pack our bag?"

"But we just got here." Her lower lip trembles.

"I know, baby, I know." Another wave of heat washes through me, making me gasp. Emma looks at me with wide, frightened eyes. "It's okay. We just need—"

A sharp knock at the door makes us both jump.

"Olivia?" A familiar voice, tight with strain. "It's Jake. Sheriff Hawkins."

I freeze, torn between relief and fresh panic. Jake. The alpha whose scent made my knees weak when I wasn't in heat. Who knows what effect he'll have now.

"Go away," I call, voice cracking.

"There are three alphas in the parking lot." His voice is controlled but urgent. "You're not safe here."

As if to emphasize his point, someone shouts from outside—crude, explicit words about what they'd like to do to the omega in heat. Emma clutches her wolf tighter, confused but sensing danger.

"I can help you." Jake's voice drops lower. "Just you and Emma. My house is safe. Please."

Another cramp doubles me over, this one so intense I bite my lip bloody to keep from crying out. I can't protect Emma like this. Can't run. Can't fight.

"Mommy?" Emma whispers. "Is the police man going to help us?"

The desperation in her voice decides me. "Yes," I say, then louder: "Jake, we need a minute."

I pull on a hoodie despite the heat scorching my skin, hoping it might contain some of my scent. Help Emma into her shoes. Grab our bag. My hands shake so badly I can barely manage the zipper.

When I open the door, the intensity of Jake's scent hits me like a physical blow. Pine and musk and alpha strength, now edged with something new—the sharp, unmistakable note of responsive rut. His pupils are blown wide, nostrils flared, but he stands a careful three feet back, hands visible at his sides. The restraint must be costing him.

"My cruiser's right here," he says, voice rough. "Can you walk?"

I nod, not trusting my voice. Emma presses against my leg, unusually quiet.

"I'll take your bag." He reaches for it, movements slow and telegraphed. When our fingers brush, electricity jolts through me, pulling a small sound from my throat that I immediately regret.

Jake's jaw clenches, but he doesn't comment. Instead, he scans the parking lot where the other alphas have grown bolder, moving closer.

"Stay behind me," he says, and then he's moving forward, placing himself between us and them.

What happens next blurs in my heat-hazed mind. Jake's voice, suddenly dropped to a growl. His posture changing, expanding somehow. Words exchanged—territory, claim, boundaries. One alpha steps forward, challenging, and Jake moves so fast I barely register it—has him by the throat, forced back against a car.

"She's under my protection," Jake snarls, all pretense of civility gone. "My town. My rules. Test me again and I'll break more than your pride."

The alpha wheezes something that must be submission because Jake releases him, turning back to us with eyes still dark with aggression. The other alphas retreat, muttering but not challenging.

"Come on." Jake ushers us to his cruiser, opening the back door. "Emma can sit up front with me."

"No." I clutch Emma closer. "She stays with me."

He nods, accepting this without argument. "Of course."

The drive passes in a haze of discomfort. Every bump in the road sends fresh waves of need through me. Jake rolls down all the windows despite the early morning chill, trying to disperse my scent, but it fills the car anyway. In the rearview mirror, I catch him white-knuckling the steering wheel, breathing through his mouth.

His house is on the outskirts of town—a simple one-story with a wide porch and thick woods behind it. Private. Isolated. Part of me notes the strategic advantages—the escape routes, the clear sightlines. The omega in heat just registers "alpha's den" and responds with a rush of slick that makes me cross my legs tighter.

"I have a guest room," Jake says as he parks. "Bathroom attached. Lock from the inside." He turns to look at me directly for the first time since the motel. "You'll be safe here, Olivia. Both of you."

The sincerity in his eyes steadies me. This close, I can see he's fighting his own biology as hard as I'm fighting mine—the flush on his neck, the slight tremor in his hands, the careful control in each movement.

"Why are you helping us?" My voice comes out huskier than intended.

His expression softens. "Because you need it. Because that's my job." A pause. "And because I can't not."

The simple honesty breaks through my haze. This isn't Marcus, using my biology against me. This is something else entirely.

"Thank you," I whisper.

"Don't thank me yet." His smile is strained. "Let's get you inside before I make promises my alpha can't keep."

Emma, quiet until now, suddenly asks, "Is Mommy going to be okay?"

Jake's eyes meet mine in the mirror, something unspoken passing between us. "Yes," he tells her with absolute certainty. "I'm going to make sure of it."

And despite everything—the heat making me weak, the danger we've fled, the risk I'm taking by trusting this alpha—I believe him.

4

—·—

J ake's guest room becomes my prison and sanctuary. The lock is sturdy, the sheets are clean, and the adjoining bathroom means I don't have to face him in the hallway with slick running down my thighs. But nothing can contain my scent completely. It seeps under the door, through the vents, announcing my fertility to the alpha whose house I've invaded. I hear him pacing at night, his footsteps heavy, restless. During the day, he maintains a careful distance, but his rut scent grows stronger—smoky and sharp, like lightning about to strike. His pupils stay dilated, his movements controlled to the point of stiffness. We orbit each other like celestial bodies, pulled by gravity but terrified of collision.

"Mommy, can I have more cereal?" Emma asks, oblivious to the tension thrumming through the kitchen.

"Sure, baby." I reach for the box, my hand trembling. Three days into my heat, and the symptoms have plateaued—still intense but manageable. Jake's been bringing me herbal teas that help dull the edge. Not as effective as suppressants, but enough that I can function.

Jake enters from the back door, fresh from his morning run. His shirt clings to his chest, damp with sweat, and the sight sends a pulse of want straight to my core. He freezes when he sees me, nostrils flaring.

"Sorry," he mutters, backing up a step. "Didn't realize you were up."

"It's your house." My voice comes out huskier than intended.

His eyes drop to my throat, where I know my scent glands are visibly swollen. He swallows hard.

"I'll shower." He turns abruptly, disappearing down the hall.

Emma watches him go, then looks at me with five-year-old directness. "Sheriff Jake smells funny."

I nearly choke on my tea. "Does he?"

She nods, serious. "Like the Christmas trees Daddy used to bring. But stronger."

The mention of Marcus—"Daddy"—twists something in my chest. Emma barely remembers him, thankfully. She was only three when we ran the first time.

"Sheriff Jake is just...different," I say carefully.

"I like him." Emma returns to her cereal. "He gave me a coloring book with police cars."

"That was nice of him." I run a hand through my tangled hair, trying to ignore the slick gathering between my thighs just from his brief presence in the room.

Jake returns twenty minutes later, hair damp, wearing a fresh shirt and jeans. His rut scent is muted but still present—pine and musk and male need.

"I called in to work," he says, keeping the kitchen island between us. "Deputy can handle things today."

The implication hangs in the air—he's staying home because of me. Because an omega in heat shouldn't be left alone with only a child for protection.

"You don't have to babysit us," I say, embarrassment making me sharp.

"It's not—" He runs a hand through his hair. "That's not what I meant."

"Can we go outside?" Emma interrupts, sensing tension. "Sheriff Jake has a tire swing!"

Jake's expression softens as he looks at her. "Of course, squirt. Just stay in the yard where I can see you, okay?"

Emma nods eagerly, abandoning her breakfast to dash for the back door.

"Shoes!" I call after her, but she's already gone.

An awkward silence falls between us. Jake busies himself making coffee, movements precise, controlled. I should return to the guest room, lock myself away until this passes. Instead, I stay, watching his hands—large, capable, gentle with Emma's cereal bowl.

"How are you feeling?" he asks, not looking at me.

"Like my skin's two sizes too small." The honesty surprises us both. "The tea helps, though. Thank you."

He nods, risking a glance. "My mother was an omega. She taught me a few things."

"Was?"

"Cancer. Three years ago."

"I'm sorry." The simple exchange feels monumental—personal details, shared history.

He shrugs, uncomfortable with sympathy. "Emma seems to be adjusting well."

"She's resilient." I watch through the window as she spins on the tire swing, her laughter carrying inside. "She's had to be."

Jake leans against the counter, coffee forgotten. "Olivia, I don't want to pry, but...is her father looking for you?"

The question sends ice through my veins despite the heat fever. "Yes."

Jake waits, not pushing, just present.

"He's not a good man." I wrap my arms around myself. "He's not safe for Emma. Or for me."

Jake's jaw tightens, a flash of alpha protectiveness crossing his face. "Is he the reason you're running?"

I nod, not trusting my voice.

"You're safe here," he says, the certainty in his tone warming something cold inside me. "Both of you."

I want to believe him. Want it so badly it scares me.

"I should check on Emma." I move toward the door, needing space from his intensity.

I don't see the spilled juice on the floor until I'm slipping. Jake moves with alpha speed, catching me before I fall. His hands grip my waist, steadying me, and the contact is electric. Heat and rut collide in a chemical reaction that steals my breath.

"Olivia." My name is a growl from his throat.

His pupils dilate fully, black swallowing blue. I can feel the tremor in his hands, the restraint costing him. My own body betrays me—omega responding to alpha, heat to rut. My scent spikes, sweet and demanding.

"Jake." I should push away, step back. Instead, my hands find his chest, feeling his heart hammer under my palm.

He lowers his head slowly, giving me time to refuse. I don't. His lips meet mine, and the world narrows to this single point of contact. The kiss is gentle for only a moment before instinct takes over. His hand slides to my neck, thumb brushing my scent gland, and I whimper into his mouth. He tastes like coffee and desire and possibility.

My back hits the counter as he presses closer, his body hard against mine. I feel the evidence of his rut against my stomach, hot and insistent. My heat responds with a rush of slick, my body preparing for what biology demands.

Emma's distant laughter breaks through the haze. I push against Jake's chest, panic cutting through desire.

"Stop." The word comes out breathless.

Jake immediately steps back, hands raised. His chest heaves, eyes still dark with want, but control reasserts itself in his posture.

"I'm sorry," he says, voice rough. "That was—"

"My fault too." I press a trembling hand to my mouth, still feeling his kiss. "I just can't. Not now. Not with—" Words fail me.

"Emma," he supplies. "And your heat affecting your choices."

That's part of it, but not all. "And my past." The admission costs me. "I'm not...ready. For what this could be."

Understanding dawns in his eyes. "He hurt you. Emma's father."

Not a question. I nod anyway, throat tight.

Jake takes another step back, deliberately creating space. "I'll wait."

Two simple words that crack something open in my chest.

"You don't even know me," I whisper.

His smile is sad, knowing. "I know enough. I know how you look at Emma. How you put yourself between her and danger without hesitation. I know you're brave and stubborn and scared." He pauses. "And I know what my instincts tell me about you."

"That I'm your mate." The words hang between us, acknowledged for the first time.

"Yes." No hesitation, no doubt. "But that doesn't mean I get to claim you. It means I get to protect you. To wait until you're ready—if you ever are."

The promise in his words staggers me. No alpha has ever offered me choice before. Protection without possession.

"I need to check on Emma," I say again, needing escape from the intensity of his gaze.

He nods, stepping aside to clear my path. "I'll be here."

As I step outside into the sunshine, watching Emma swing higher and higher, I realize Jake's promise has done something dangerous—it's given me hope. Hope that there might be an alpha who sees me as more than an omega to possess. Hope that Emma and I might find safety that doesn't require constant running.

Hope is the most dangerous thing for a woman like me. But as I hear Jake moving in the kitchen, his scent wrapping around me even from a distance, I can't help clinging to it anyway.

5

My heat breaks on the fifth day, fading like a fever that's run its course. The relief is immediate and overwhelming—to be in my own skin again, to think clearly without biology clouding every thought. The embarrassment follows just as quickly. I've invaded Jake's home, filled it with my scent, pushed his alpha instincts to the breaking point, and then rejected him. I expect awkwardness, perhaps resentment. Instead, Jake brings me coffee in the kitchen and asks if I'm ready to see what Sanctuary has to offer. His eyes are clear now, the rut-darkness gone, but something else remains—a steady warmth when he looks at me that's almost harder to face.

"I should find our own place," I say, cupping the mug between my palms. "We've imposed enough."

Jake leans against the counter, casual in a way that wasn't possible during my heat. "No rush. Besides, Emma's become attached to the tire swing."

Through the window, I watch my daughter spinning in lazy circles, content in a way I haven't seen in too long.

"About the diner job," Jake continues. "Marge is expecting you this afternoon if you're feeling up to it."

I turn to him, surprised. "You didn't tell me you spoke to her."

He shrugs, almost sheepish. "Wanted to have good news when your heat broke. The pay's decent, tips are better, and she'll work around Emma's schedule."

The thoughtfulness of it strikes me speechless. Marcus never concerned himself with practical matters like how I would earn money or care for our child. Those were omega concerns, beneath him.

"Thank you," I manage finally.

"There's more." He slides a pamphlet across the counter. "Sanctuary Elementary. They've got space in their kindergarten class. Emma could start Monday if you want."

I pick up the glossy brochure, something tight squeezing in my chest. A job. A school. The trappings of a normal life I've barely dared imagine.

"This is..." I trail off, unable to express how much it means.

"Just the basics," Jake says, misreading my emotion as disappointment. "We can look at apartments next—"

"No, it's perfect." My voice catches. "It's just been a long time since anyone helped us like this."

Something flashes in his eyes—anger, not at me but for me. He doesn't push for details about Marcus, and I'm grateful.

"Small towns," he says instead, his tone deliberately lighter. "Everyone helps each other."

"Is that why you became sheriff?" I ask, genuinely curious.

His smile turns wry. "Family tradition. My father was sheriff before me. His father before him."

"A dynasty of law enforcement."

"Something like that." He glances at Emma through the window. "I was thinking of taking her fishing this afternoon. There's a pond on the property. If that's okay with you."

The question—his deference to my authority as Emma's mother—warms me more than I want to admit.

"She'd love that."

The diner interview with Marge is barely an interview at all. She looks me up and down, asks if I can carry plates and ignore drunk idiots on weekend nights, then hands me an apron.

"Sheriff vouched for you," she says, as if that settles everything. "Start tomorrow, 7 AM. Bring the kid if you need to."

Just like that, I have a job. When I return to Jake's house, I find him and Emma by the small pond behind the property, fishing poles in hand. I hang back, watching them unnoticed.

"You gotta be patient," Jake is saying, his voice gentle but not patronizing. "Fish aren't in any hurry."

Emma's face is scrunched in concentration, her small hands gripping the child-sized pole. "How do they breathe underwater?"

"They have special organs called gills," Jake explains. "They take oxygen from the water, kind of like how we take it from the air."

"That's weird," Emma declares, making Jake laugh.

"Nature's full of weird stuff, squirt. That's what makes it interesting."

The easy way he talks to her—not talking down, not dismissing her questions—makes my heart clench. Marcus never had patience for Emma's curiosity. Children, especially female ones, were to be seen and not heard in his pack.

Emma suddenly squeals as her line goes taut. "I got one!"

Jake moves behind her, hands steadying hers but letting her do the work. "Easy now, reel slow and steady."

I watch my daughter's face transform with triumph as she pulls in a small sunfish, Jake's larger hands helping her without taking over.

"Mommy, look!" Emma spots me and holds up her prize. "I caught a fish!"

"I see that!" I move closer, genuinely impressed. "You're a natural."

Jake helps her remove the hook and release the fish back into the pond. "Always throw the little ones back so they can grow bigger," he tells her solemnly.

Emma watches the fish swim away, then looks up at Jake with complete trust. "Can we do this again tomorrow?"

"Anytime you want, squirt." He ruffles her hair, and she doesn't pull away—another small miracle.

Later, after Emma is tucked into bed in the guest room, I find Jake on the back porch, nursing a beer and watching the stars. I hesitate, then join him, accepting the bottle he offers.

"Got the job," I say, taking a small sip. "Thanks to you."

"Marge needed help. You needed work." He shrugs off the credit. "Emma had fun today."

"I saw." I turn the bottle between my fingers. "She likes you."

"She's a great kid." His voice softens. "Smart. Asks good questions."

"She doesn't usually warm up to people. Especially men." I don't need to explain why.

Jake nods, understanding the unspoken. "Trust has to be earned."

"Yes, it does." I look at him sideways. "You're good with her."

"My sister has kids. I get practice at being the fun uncle." He glances at me. "Emma said you enrolled her in school today."

"Monday." The word feels significant—a commitment to staying, at least for a while. "I put down your address. Hope that's okay. I'll find us a place soon."

"No rush," he says again, and I wonder if he means it or if he's just being kind.

We sit in comfortable silence, watching fireflies wink in the gathering darkness. It feels domestic, peaceful—dangerous in its normalcy.

"Tell me about Sanctuary," I say, needing to break the spell before I sink too deeply into it. "The real version, not the tourist brochure."

Jake smiles, leaning back in his chair. "Born and raised here. Population nine hundred and twelve as of last census. Nothing much happens except the occasional drunk tourist or teenage prank." His voice takes on a storytelling quality. "Main Street hasn't changed in fifty years. Everyone knows everyone's business. The diner has the best pie in three counties, but don't tell Marge I said so or she'll raise the prices."

I laugh despite myself. "Sounds idyllic."

"It can be." He looks at me directly. "It could be for you and Emma too."

The simple statement hits me with unexpected force. A home. A community. Safety. All the things I've been running toward for years.

"Maybe," I allow, not ready to commit more than that. "One day at a time."

He accepts this with a nod, not pushing. Another point in his favor.

As we sit there, stars multiplying in the darkness above us, I realize I'm falling for this man—this alpha who asks instead of demands, who sees me as a person first and an omega second. It terrifies me how easily I could build a life here, with him. How simple it would be to trust him completely.

And that's exactly why I need to be careful. The last time I trusted an alpha, it nearly destroyed me. Jake seems different—feels different—but so did Marcus, once.

Still, as I glance at Jake's profile in the moonlight, something in me whispers that maybe, just maybe, Sanctuary might live up to its name after all.

6

—.—

The Sanctuary Founder's Day Festival transforms the town square into a swirl of carnival games, food stands, and twinkle lights strung between trees. Two weeks since my heat ended, and I'm almost starting to believe we could belong here. Emma darts between booths, face sticky with cotton candy, more carefree than I've seen her in years. I've been working at the diner, saving tips in a coffee can, and the locals have stopped watching me like I'm about to steal the silverware. Progress. Small-town integration. Jake stands across the square with a group of deputies, laughing at something. He hasn't pushed, hasn't pressured. Just steady presence, respectful distance. It's making it harder, not easier, to keep my guard up.

"Mommy, can I play the duck game?" Emma tugs at my hand, pointing to a booth where children are fishing for plastic ducks in a kiddie pool.

"Sure, baby." I hand the teenage attendant a ticket and watch Emma's face scrunch in concentration as she selects her duck.

"She's settling in well."

I jump at Jake's voice behind me, then try to hide my reaction. "You're sneaky for someone so large."

He grins, not taking offense. "Sheriff training. How's the festival?"

"Nice." I gesture to Emma who's triumphantly claiming a small stuffed bear prize. "She's having fun."

"And you?" His eyes search mine, always looking deeper than I want him to.

I shrug. "It's… normal. Been a while since we had normal."

Something in my tone must betray me because his expression softens. "Normal can take getting used to."

Emma runs back, clutching her prize. "Sheriff Jake! Look what I won!"

"That's quite a bear," he says seriously. "Very impressive."

She beams up at him. "Can I go on the bouncy castle?"

I check my watch. "One more hour, then we need to head home. It's getting late."

"I can take her," Jake offers. "If you want to enjoy the festival without kid duty for a bit."

The offer is tempting. I haven't had a moment to myself in... I can't remember how long.

"Are you sure?"

"Positive." He holds out his hand to Emma. "What do you say, squirt? Ready to show me your bouncing skills?"

Emma takes his hand without hesitation, a trust that makes my chest ache. "I can bounce higher than anyone!"

"I believe it." He glances back at me. "We'll meet you by the lemonade stand in an hour?"

I nod, watching them walk away, Emma chattering up at him. Something warm and dangerous unfurls in my chest at the sight.

Half an hour later, I'm browsing a booth of handmade soaps when Marge from the diner spots me.

"Olivia! Thank god. We're running low on napkins and cups for the lemonade stand. Jake's got the key to the storage shed behind the community center. Can you find him and get them? My feet are killing me."

"Sure." I abandon the soaps and head toward the bouncy castle, but Jake and Emma aren't there.

I spot them by the face-painting booth, Emma now sporting a butterfly across her cheeks, Jake patiently holding her stuffed animals.

"Marge needs supplies from the storage shed," I explain after Emma shows off her face. "She said you have the key?"

"I do." He checks his watch. "Emma, what do you say we drop you with Mrs. Wilson at the cookie booth while your mom and I get supplies? She said you could help decorate."

Emma's eyes light up. "Can I, Mommy?"

"Of course." I smooth her hair. "We'll be right back."

After settling Emma with the grandmotherly woman at the cookie booth, Jake leads me behind the community center to a small shed tucked against the trees. The festival sounds fade slightly here, replaced by cricket song and the rustle of leaves.

"Should be quick," Jake says, unlocking the padlock. "Just napkins and cups, right?"

The shed is smaller than it appeared from outside—barely ten feet square, filled with folding chairs, boxes of decorations, and festival supplies. Jake flicks on a single bulb hanging from the ceiling, casting everything in dim yellow light.

"Napkins should be on that shelf." He points, moving toward a stack of boxes labeled 'cups'.

I squeeze past him, acutely aware of his body heat in the confined space. The scent of him—pine and male and now-familiar alpha—fills my nostrils. Two weeks of careful distance, and now we're practically pressed together.

"Found them," I say, my voice oddly breathless as I reach for the napkin packages.

A sudden gust of wind slams the shed door shut behind us.

Jake turns, frowning. "That's not good."

"Why?" I move toward the door, suddenly claustrophobic.

He tries the handle. "This lock automatically engages. That's why I had the key." He pats his pockets. "Which is currently..."

"Outside," I finish, seeing the key still dangling from the exterior lock through the small window.

"I'll call for help." Jake pulls out his phone, then grimaces. "No signal."

"Perfect." I lean against the wall, trying not to panic. Small spaces have never bothered me, but small spaces with alphas... that's different.

Jake keeps his distance, moving to the opposite wall. "Someone will notice we're missing soon. Emma will ask for you."

"True." I wrap my arms around myself, suddenly cold despite the warm evening.

Minutes tick by in awkward silence. Jake shifts, and in the small space, his scent intensifies—pine and musk and something new. Something responding to my proximity.

"Jake." My voice comes out as a warning.

"I know." His jaw is tight, eyes careful. "Your scent is… it's stronger in here."

The realization hits me—we're locked in a small space, scents concentrated, pheromones building. My body responds traitorously, a familiar warmth kindling low in my belly.

"It's the mate pull," I whisper, naming it for the first time since that kiss in his kitchen.

He nods, not denying it. "I can control it."

"I know you can." And I do know. He's proven his restraint repeatedly.

Maybe that's why I take a step toward him instead of away.

His pupils dilate instantly. "Olivia."

"I'm not in heat," I say, needing him to understand. "This is just me."

Something flashes in his eyes—hope, hunger, uncertainty. "Are you sure?"

Another step closer. The air between us thickens with tension and possibility. "I'm scared," I admit. "Not of you. Of this. Of what it means."

Jake doesn't move, letting me come to him. "Tell me what you want."

The question—so simple, so revolutionary. What I want, not what I should do or what's expected of me.

"Touch me," I whisper. "Please."

His control breaks beautifully. One moment he's still, the next his hands are cupping my face, his mouth claiming mine with a hunger that steals my breath. This kiss is nothing like our first—that was biology, heat and rut. This is choice. Deliberate. Searing.

I press against him, hands clutching his shirt, opening to him as his tongue sweeps into my mouth. He tastes like lemonade and desire and possibility. His hands slide down my body, lifting me effortlessly until my legs wrap around his waist, back pressed against the shed wall.

"Tell me to stop and I will," he growls against my throat, lips finding my pulse point.

"Don't stop." I tilt my head, offering access to my scent glands—an omega's ultimate submission.

He groans, the sound vibrating through me as he nuzzles the sensitive spot, then licks across it. Pleasure shoots straight to my core, slick gathering between my thighs. I rock against the hard length of him, already fully aroused.

"Olivia." My name is a prayer and curse on his lips. "I need—"

"Yes," I cut him off. "Anything."

His hands are everywhere then—under my shirt, caressing my breasts, thumbs circling my nipples until I'm gasping. My own hands grow bold, exploring the muscles of his chest, his back, dipping below his waistband to feel the heated skin beneath.

Clothing becomes an obstacle. We fumble with buttons, zippers, urgency making us clumsy. When he finally slides his hand between my thighs, finding me wet and ready, we both moan.

"You're perfect," he whispers, sliding two fingers inside me, his thumb circling my clit with devastating precision. "So perfect for me."

I come apart embarrassingly quickly, clenching around his fingers, biting his shoulder to muffle my cries. Before I've fully recovered, he's lifting me again, positioning me.

"Protection?" he manages to ask, his control hanging by a thread.

"I'm on birth control," I gasp. "Clean. You?"

"Clean." His eyes meet mine, waiting for final permission.

I answer by guiding him to my entrance, sinking down onto him in one fluid motion. The stretch is exquisite—it's been so long, and he's larger than I expected. We both freeze, adjusting, foreheads pressed together, sharing breath.

"Mine," he whispers, the word slipping out unbidden.

And instead of fear, I feel completion. "Yours," I agree, rocking my hips.

There's a moment—a heartbeat—when we just breathe each other in, suspended in the liquid gold light and the scent-thick air, and then Jake moves. The first thrust is careful, reverent, a question.

I answer with my whole body, arching into him, my hips meeting his. He groans, one broad palm bracing my jaw, the other gripping my thigh to anchor me higher, tighter, so I can't help but yield.

The world collapses to the pulse between my legs and the heat of his mouth devouring mine. My back scrapes against particleboard, but I don't care. He fills me so perfectly, the pressure almost sweet enough to cry out. Each time he drives deeper, it peels away another layer of my fear, another memory of nights spent bracing for the wrong hands and the wrong scent and the wrong, wrong, wrong. With Jake, there's only this: the dizzying rightness of being wanted, being chosen, being claimed on my own terms.

He fucks me like he's starving. Every instinct he's banked for weeks pours out—his teeth skimming my jaw, his tongue at my ear, both hands never gentle for long. I bite his shoulder, not breaking the skin, and he shudders. His scent spikes, wild and piney and unmistakably alpha, and I feel my own body bloom in answer, omega pheromones flooding the cramped shed until we're both drunk on it.

I want him to break me open, and he does. My legs locked around his waist, I take everything he gives—harder now, almost punishing, but never crossing the unspoken line. My fingernails leave half-moons in his skin. He pistons into me, breath ragged, eyes gone feral-black, and I can feel the pulse of his knot at the base, swelling with each thrust.

My body responds, sharp and bright. Slick gushes; I'm soaked and aching and desperate. I dig my fingers into his hair, yanking him down to my neck, daring him to take what he wants. His mouth finds my gland, and when he nips—not enough to mark, but enough to promise—I shatter, coming hard and sudden, the force of it ripping a cry from my throat.

He doesn't stop. He can't. He chases my high, chasing his own, hips slamming into me with frantic need. I can feel the thickening at the base of his cock, the primal urge to tie, and some deep-rooted part of me that always dreaded this moment instead opens up like a flower to sunlight.

I'm not afraid. Not with him.
When his knot begins to swell, pressing against my entrance, I expect panic. Instead, I feel only rightness.

"Please," I beg, not knowing exactly what I'm asking for.

Jake's eyes meet mine, wild with desire but still seeking consent. "It might hurt."

"I don't care." I kiss him, fierce and claiming. "Make me yours."

With a growl that raises goosebumps along my skin, he pushes his knot inside me, stretching me to the point of sweet pain. The pressure against every sensitive spot triggers another orgasm, more intense than the others. I cry out his name as he follows me over the edge, his release pulsing hot inside me.

Connected, locked together, we slide to the floor, Jake cradling me in his lap. His lips find my neck, teeth grazing my mating gland but not biting—not yet. That final step waits for another time, a conscious choice outside this haze of pleasure.

Reality returns slowly. The hard floor beneath us. The faint sounds of the festival. The fact that we're still locked in a storage shed, my daughter waiting somewhere outside.

"That was…" I trail off, unable to find words.

Jake's arms tighten around me. "Unexpected?"

I laugh softly. "Understatement."

He brushes hair from my face, expression turning serious. "I don't regret it."

"Neither do I." And it's true. Despite the complications, despite my fears, this feels right in a way nothing has before.

His knot eventually subsides, allowing us to separate. We dress in awkward silence, the small space now filled with the mingled scent of sex and satisfaction.

"Someone will come looking for us soon," Jake says, straightening my shirt with gentle hands.

As if summoned by his words, voices call from outside. "Sheriff? You in there?"

Jake moves to the window. "We're locked in, Mike. Key's in the door."

Moments later, the door swings open, revealing one of Jake's deputies, who takes in our disheveled appearance with a quickly concealed smirk.

"Emma's asking for you both," he says, professional enough not to comment further. "Mrs. Wilson's been keeping her busy, but she's getting anxious."

Guilt hits me hard. "We'll be right there. Thank you."

As we walk back toward the festival, cups and napkins forgotten, Jake catches my hand. "We should talk about this. About what it means."

I know what he's asking—where we go from here, what we are to each other now.

"Yes," I agree. "But first, Emma."

He nods, understanding as always. But before we rejoin the crowd, he pulls me close one more time, his scent wrapping around me like a promise.

"Whatever you decide, whatever you need," he whispers against my hair, "I'm here. All in."

The simple declaration terrifies and thrills me in equal measure. For the first time since running from Marcus, I want to stop running altogether. I want to stay, to build something real with this man who asks instead of takes, who sees me as an equal, not a possession.

But as we find Emma, her face lighting up at the sight of us, reality crashes back. Marcus is still out there. The danger hasn't passed just because I've found happiness. In fact, I may have just complicated everything beyond repair.

The mate bond thrums between Jake and me, new but undeniable. There's no going back now. Whatever comes next, we'll face it together—for better or worse.

7

Three days after the festival, I'm refilling coffee cups at the diner when the bells above the door jingle. I don't look up immediately—the lunch rush is just starting, and Marge has me working the counter and two tables near the window. It's the sudden silence that gets my attention. Conversations stop mid-sentence. Forks pause halfway to mouths. And that's when I smell it—the scent that's haunted my nightmares for two years. Smoky, with undertones of whiskey and something metallic like blood. My body freezes, coffee pot suspended over a customer's cup, as Marcus steps into the diner, flanked by two of his pack enforcers. His eyes find mine instantly, his smile spreading slow and predatory across his handsome face.

"There's my girl," he says, voice carrying in the silent diner. "Been looking everywhere for you, Livie."

The coffee pot slips from my numb fingers, crashing to the floor. Hot liquid splashes my legs, but I barely feel it. All I can think is: Emma. Thank god she's at school. Safe, for now.

"Clumsy as ever." Marcus clicks his tongue, stepping over the spill as he approaches the counter. His enforcers flank out, positioning themselves near the door. Blocking escape.

I back up until I hit the wall, fingers scrabbling for anything that might serve as a weapon. "How did you find me?"

He leans against the counter, casual as if we're catching up after a brief separation. "Credit card trail. Sloppy, Livie. You know better." His eyes sweep over me, lingering on my neck where Jake's scent still clings despite my shower this morning. His nostrils flare. "Been busy, I see."

Marge appears from the kitchen, wiping her hands on her apron. "Everything alright here, Olivia?"

"Fine," I say automatically, protecting her. Marcus wouldn't hesitate to hurt anyone who interferes.

"Actually," Marcus turns his charming smile on her, "I'm here to collect my mate and daughter. Family business."

"Ex-mate," I correct, finding my voice. "And you have no right to Emma."

His smile doesn't falter, but his eyes go hard. "Now, Livie. Let's not air our dirty laundry in public." He reaches across the counter for my wrist. "Come on. Let's go somewhere private and talk about this like adults."

I jerk back from his touch. "There's nothing to talk about. I'm not going anywhere with you."

The bell over the door jingles again, and relief crashes through me as Jake steps in, immediately assessing the situation. His eyes lock with mine first—a silent question. Are you okay? I give him the smallest nod.

"Problem here?" Jake asks, voice deceptively casual as he moves further into the diner.

Marcus turns, sizing Jake up with a predator's calculating gaze. "No problem. Just collecting what's mine."

"Nothing in this diner belongs to you," Jake says, stepping closer. "Especially not Olivia or Emma."

Marcus's fake charm vanishes. "And who the fuck are you?"

"Sheriff Jake Hawkins." He doesn't flash his badge or emphasize his title. He doesn't need to. His authority fills the room, his scent sharpening with protective fury. "And you're in my town."

"Cute." Marcus snorts. "Playing sheriff and savior to my runaway omega. Did she tell you she's already mated? That she stole my daughter?"

"I'm not your mate," I say, hands curling into fists. "The arrangement was forced. You know that."

Jake's expression doesn't change, but I see his jaw tighten. "Arranged mating? That's been illegal in this state for fifteen years."

"Our pack has traditional values," Marcus says smoothly. "Olivia's father and I came to an understanding. All perfectly above board."

"My father sold me to pay gambling debts," I snap, past caring about public exposure. "I was seventeen. He was thirty-five. There was nothing traditional about it."

Murmurs ripple through the diner. Several customers slip out phones, texting rapidly. The town gossip network activating in real time.

Marcus's pleasant mask slips further. "Enough drama, Olivia. Get your things. We're leaving. Emma too."

"No." I step around the counter, positioning myself beside Jake. "Emma is my daughter. Mine. And we're staying right here."

Marcus laughs, the sound ugly and familiar. "With him? Your new alpha plaything? How long before he gets bored with damaged goods?"

Jake moves so fast I barely register it—one moment he's beside me, the next he has Marcus by the throat, shoving him against the nearest wall. The two enforcers start forward, but Marge's cook and two burly customers block their path.

"Listen carefully," Jake growls, his voice dropped to that alpha register that raises goosebumps on my arms. "Olivia is my mate. Emma is under my protection. You threaten either of them, you deal with me."

Marcus struggles against Jake's grip, face reddening. "She... can't be... your mate," he chokes out. "Not fully... No bite..."

Jake releases him, stepping back. "That's her choice to make. Not yours. Not mine."

Marcus straightens, rubbing his throat, eyes darting between us. Understanding dawns in his expression. "You haven't claimed her yet. Not officially." He laughs again. "Then she's still mine by law. First claim."

"Bullshit," Jake says flatly. "Forced matings aren't recognized here. Neither are pack 'arrangements' that violate state law."

"It'll be my word against hers." Marcus straightens his jacket. "And who do you think the courts will believe? A respected alpha businessman with a spotless record, or a runaway omega with a history of instability?"

My stomach drops. He's right. Without proof of abuse, without witnesses, the legal system often sides with alphas. Especially wealthy ones.

"They'll believe her," comes a voice from across the diner. Marge steps forward, phone in hand. "Because I just got off the phone with Sheriff Daniels from Canton County. Seems you've got outstanding warrants there, Mr. Wilson. Domestic violence. Coercion. Three other omegas have come forward since Olivia left."

Marcus's face contorts with rage. "You interfering bitch—"

"Careful," Jake warns, his hand moving to his hip where his service weapon rests. "That's strike two."

I stare at Marge in shock. How long has she known? How has she been helping me without my knowledge?

Marcus's enforcers shift uneasily, reading the room. The diner has filled with more locals—word spreading quickly through town. They form a loose circle around us, faces grim and determined.

"This isn't just about Olivia anymore," Jake says, voice level. "This is about my town. My people. We protect our own here."

The simple declaration brings a lump to my throat. Our own. After years of running, of being nobody's, the claim feels like shelter.

Marcus's eyes narrow as he calculates odds. Three against twenty isn't favorable, even for alphas. "This isn't over," he says finally. "We're staying at the motel outside town. I expect to see my daughter tomorrow, or I'll file kidnapping charges."

"Your name isn't on her birth certificate," I counter, finding strength in Jake's steady presence beside me. "You have no legal claim to her."

"We'll see about that." Marcus straightens his jacket again, a gesture I remember from countless confrontations. His way of regaining control. "Pack law still holds weight. My pack will back my claim."

"Not in my jurisdiction," Jake says. "Now, I suggest you leave before I find a reason to arrest you."

For a tense moment, I think Marcus will push it further. Then he signals to his men. "Tomorrow, Livie. We'll finish this conversation then." His eyes shift to Jake. "Enjoy her while you can, Sheriff. She's entertaining enough, but high maintenance. Not worth the trouble."

The casual cruelty, so familiar it barely stings anymore, hangs in the air as they leave. The bell jingles with bitter cheerfulness as the door closes behind them.

My legs give out. Jake catches me before I hit the floor, guiding me to a chair. The diner erupts in concerned voices, questions, offers of help.

"Emma," I gasp, panic returning. "He knows about Emma. He'll go to the school—"

"Already handled," Marge says, showing me her phone. "Texted the principal while you were facing down that bastard. Deputy's already there. Emma's safe."

Jake crouches before me, his hands warm on mine. "We need to get you both somewhere secure. My place. Until we figure this out."

I nod, too shaken to argue. "He won't give up. He hates losing. Especially to another alpha."

"Then he's really going to hate what happens next," Jake says, his voice deceptively calm. But I catch the edge underneath—pure alpha rage, barely contained. "Because I'm not letting him near you or Emma ever again."

Looking into his eyes, seeing the absolute certainty there, I almost believe him. But I've underestimated Marcus before. The fact that he found us at all proves how relentless he can be.

"I'm sorry," I whisper, aware of the curious eyes watching us. "I never meant to bring this to your door. To your town."

Jake's expression softens. "This isn't on you. None of it."

As he helps me stand, the diner patrons close ranks around us. Offers of help pour in—places to stay, legal contacts, even weapons. This town of strangers suddenly transformed into allies.

"Let's get Emma," I say, finding strength in their support. "And then we plan."

Jake's hand finds mine, squeezing gently. "Together."

The simple word contains a promise that terrifies and strengthens me in equal measure. For the first time since Marcus entered my life, I'm not facing him alone.

But as Jake leads me out to his cruiser, I can't shake the feeling that this is only the beginning. Marcus has found us once. And he won't stop until he gets what he wants—or until someone stops him permanently.

8

—·—

Night falls like a shroud over Jake's house. Emma sleeps fitfully in the guest room, exhausted from the fear and confusion of being rushed from school to safety. Jake moves through the house, checking locks, making calls, his shoulders a rigid line of tension. I sit at the kitchen table, a cup of tea gone cold between my palms, replaying Marcus's words on endless loop. My fault. All of it. I've dragged Jake and this entire town into my nightmare. Marcus won't stop. He'll hurt anyone who stands between him and what he considers his property—me and Emma. Running is what I know. It's kept us alive for two years. And now it's time to run again, before anyone else gets hurt because of me.

"Deputy Mills will take the first watch tonight," Jake says, returning to the kitchen. "Rotations every four hours. The station's keeping eyes on Marcus and his men at the motel."

I nod mechanically. Jake has been in sheriff mode since the diner, efficient and controlled, but I catch the fury simmering beneath—in the tightness around his eyes, the way his hands clench when he thinks I'm not looking.

"You should try to sleep," he says, softer now. "Tomorrow we'll figure out next steps."

"Right." I force a smile that feels like shattered glass. "Sleep."

Jake studies me, seeing too much. He always does. "Olivia—"

"I'm fine." I stand abruptly, needing escape from his perceptiveness. "Just tired. You're right."

He doesn't believe me, but he doesn't push. Another gift—the space to have my secrets, my fears. "I'll be right out here if you need anything."

In the guest room, I curl around Emma's sleeping form, breathing in her sweet child-scent. She clutches her stuffed wolf, mumbling in her sleep. For two years, it's been just us against the world. Moving from town to town, never settling, never safe enough. Until Sanctuary. Until Jake.

And now I've put them all in danger.

I wait until the house settles into night silence. Jake's soft snores drift from the living room couch. The deputy's car idles at the end of the driveway, a watchful presence.

Three AM. The witching hour. Time for hard choices.

I slip from bed, careful not to wake Emma. Our duffel bag is still half-packed from our hasty move to Jake's. I add the few items we've accumulated—Emma's school papers, her new coloring books from Jake, my diner uniform. The life we almost had, reduced to a single bag again.

Cash is the problem. I have some saved from the diner, but not enough for bus tickets far enough away. I'll need to risk the ATM in the next town over.

A floorboard creaks behind me. I whirl, heart in my throat.

Jake stands in the doorway, barefoot and rumpled with sleep, eyes sharp with understanding. "Going somewhere?"

I clutch a shirt to my chest like it might shield me from his gaze. "I have to."

"No, you don't." His voice is gentle but firm. "You're safer here, with people who can protect you."

"No one is safe with Marcus around." The shirt twists in my hands. "You don't know what he's capable of."

"Then tell me." He doesn't move closer, giving me space. "Help me understand."

The words pour out before I can stop them. "He burned down the apartment of an omega who helped me the first time I ran. Just to send a message. He broke his own brother's arm for giving me a ride to the bus station." My voice cracks. "He has money, connections. People who owe him favors. The law doesn't stop men like him."

Jake absorbs this, his face grim. "And you think running will solve this? He found you once. He'll find you again."

"Maybe. But you'll be safe. This town will be safe." I look away, unable to bear the intensity of his gaze. "I won't have your blood on my hands."

"And what about Emma?" His question cuts to the heart of it. "Another school? Another life uprooted? Always looking over your shoulder?"

"She's used to it." The words taste bitter. "She'll adjust."

"She shouldn't have to." Jake takes a step forward, then stops himself. "She deserves stability. A home. People who love her."

"You think I don't know that?" My voice rises before I remember Emma sleeping nearby. "You think I want this life for her? I don't have a choice!"

"Yes, you do." His certainty infuriates me. "You can choose to stay. To fight. With me. With this town behind you."

I shake my head, throat tight with unshed tears. "I can't risk it. I can't risk you."

"That's my choice to make." Another step closer. "Not yours."

"Why?" I demand, anger flaring through fear. "Why would you risk everything for us? You barely know me."

"Because I love you." The simple declaration lands like a physical blow. "Both of you. And that's not the mate bond talking. That's just me, Olivia. I love your strength, your fierce protection of Emma, your quiet determination. I love the way you hum when you think no one's listening, how you always check Emma's homework twice, how you face each day despite everything you've been through."

Tears spill down my cheeks. "Jake—"

"I know it's fast," he continues, relentless in his honesty. "I know it's complicated. But some things you just know. And I know that you and Emma belong here, with me. We can face Marcus together. We can win."

"You don't know that." My voice breaks on the words.

"No, I don't," he admits. "But I know running isn't the answer. It just postpones the inevitable. And it means he wins."

A small sound from the bed interrupts us. Emma sits up, rubbing her eyes, taking in the packed bag, my tear-streaked face.

"Are we leaving again?" Her voice is small, fearful.

"No, baby, we're just—" I can't finish the lie.

"I don't want to go." Emma's lower lip trembles. "I like it here. I like my school and Miss Wilson and my friends. And I like Sheriff Jake."

Jake's expression softens as he looks at her. "I like you too, squirt."

Emma clutches her stuffed wolf tighter. "Is the bad man making us leave?"

The question guts me. After everything, she still knows when we're running from danger. No child should have that awareness.

"No one's making us do anything," I say carefully. "Mommy's just trying to keep everyone safe."

"But Sheriff Jake keeps people safe." She says it with such certainty, such faith. "That's his job. He told me."

Jake kneels beside the bed, eye level with her. "That's right. And I promise I'll do everything I can to keep you and your mom safe."

"See?" Emma looks at me triumphantly. "We don't have to go."

I look between them—my daughter and the man who's become so essential to us both in such a short time. The man who's offering us not just protection, but a real home. A family.

"Please, Mommy." Emma's eyes fill with tears. "Please don't make us leave Sheriff Daddy."

The slip—"Sheriff Daddy"—lands like a thunderbolt. Jake's breath catches, his eyes meeting mine over Emma's head, emotion raw on his face.

My legs give out. I sink to the floor, the fight draining from me. "Emma, honey, Jake isn't—"

"I could be," Jake interrupts softly. "If that's what you both want."

The offer hangs in the air between us—not just protection, not just temporary safety, but permanence. Family. Home.

Everything I've never dared want for myself. Everything I've desperately wanted for Emma.

"The bad man hurt you before," Emma says with five-year-old directness. "Sheriff Daddy won't let him hurt you again."

"It's not that simple, baby." But even as I say it, I feel my resolve weakening.

Jake moves to sit beside me on the floor, careful not to touch me, respecting my space even now. "Maybe it is that simple. Stay. Let me—let us—help you fight this. No more running."

I look at my packed bag, at Emma's hopeful face, at Jake's steady presence. The omega in me wants to flee from danger—it's instinct, preservation. But the mother in me wants stability for my child. And the woman in me... she wants what Jake is offering. A partner. A mate who sees me as an equal, not a possession.

"If we stay," I say slowly, "if we fight... I need to know Emma will be protected no matter what happens to me."

"Nothing will happen to you," Jake says fiercely.

"Promise me anyway." I need this certainty, this foundation.

His eyes hold mine, absolute in their conviction. "I promise. Emma will always be safe, always have a home, no matter what."

Emma scrambles off the bed, throwing herself into our laps, arms trying to encircle us both. "See? We can stay forever now."

Forever. Such an impossible word. But looking at Jake's face, at Emma's hope, I allow myself to believe it might be possible.

"Okay," I whisper, the decision settling into my bones. "We stay. We fight."

Jake's hand finds mine, squeezing gently. "Together."

The word echoes in the quiet room. Not alone anymore. Together.

For the first time since Marcus entered my life, I choose to stand my ground instead of run. For Emma. For Jake. For myself.

9

—·—

Morning brings a strange calm. Jake's house transforms into command central—deputies coming and going, maps spread across the kitchen table, radios crackling with updates on Marcus's movements. Emma stays in the guest room with a deputy's wife, distracted with games and stories. I move through it all in a fog of anticipation, adrenaline thrumming beneath my skin. This confrontation has been coming for two years. Every town, every midnight escape, every moment looking over my shoulder—all leading to this day. I should be terrified, but a curious strength fills me instead. No more running. No more hiding. Today, Marcus loses his power over me, one way or another.

"They've checked out of the motel," Jake announces, hanging up his phone. "Three vehicles. Heading this way."

His deputies exchange glances, hands moving instinctively to their weapons. Jake shakes his head.

"No guns unless absolutely necessary. This is pack business first."

"Pack business?" I ask, surprised. Jake hasn't mentioned being part of a formal pack structure.

"My father was Alpha of Sanctuary Pack before me," Jake explains, catching my confusion. "I took over when he died. It's not something we advertise to outsiders, but every wolf in town knows the hierarchy."

This revelation shifts something in my understanding of him—the natural authority, the town's immediate rallying around us yesterday. It wasn't just because he's sheriff. It's because he's their Alpha.

"You never said—"

"It didn't seem important." He shrugs. "Pack politics isn't why you're here. But it might be what saves us today."

A deputy by the window stiffens. "They're here. Three cars. At least eight wolves."

Jake nods, unsurprised. "More than yesterday. He's making a statement." He turns to me, eyes serious. "Stay inside with Emma. No matter what happens."

"Jake—"

"Please." His voice softens. "I need to know you're safe."

I want to argue, to stand beside him, but the thought of Emma witnessing violence—possibly losing another parent figure—stops me. I nod reluctantly.

Jake leads his deputies outside, forming a line across the front of the property. I watch through the window as Marcus's caravan stops at the edge of the driveway. Car doors slam. Marcus emerges from the lead vehicle, his enforcers flanking him. Five more men exit the other cars—large, rough-looking alphas with the hard eyes of men accustomed to violence.

Despite the closed windows, their voices carry.

"Quite the welcome committee, Sheriff," Marcus calls, sauntering forward. "All this for little old me?"

"You were told to leave town," Jake responds, his stance relaxed but alert. "Instead, you brought reinforcements. That tells me you're not here to talk."

Marcus spreads his hands in mock innocence. "Just insurance. In case you've forgotten how pack law works when it comes to mated pairs."

"Pack law doesn't supersede state law," Jake counters. "And it definitely doesn't apply to forced matings."

"There was nothing forced about it." Marcus's false charm drops, his voice hardening. "Olivia's father and I had an arrangement. She knew her duty."

"Selling a seventeen-year-old to pay gambling debts isn't an arrangement," Jake says, his control slipping for the first time. "It's trafficking."

Marcus laughs, the sound scraping across my nerves like broken glass. "Such dramatic language. She was well-treated, given a nice home, provided for. Until she got ideas above her station."

Through the window, I see Jake's hands clench into fists. His scent must be spiking with rage because Marcus's enforcers shift uneasily.

"Last chance," Jake says, voice deadly quiet. "Leave town. Leave Olivia and Emma alone. Or face the consequences."

"Or what?" Marcus scoffs. "You'll arrest me? On what charges? I have every right to reclaim my mate and child."

"Not here. Not in my territory."

"Ah, now we get to it." Marcus's smile turns predatory. "Territory. The real issue. You've scented what's mine, and now you want to keep her."

"Olivia belongs to herself," Jake says firmly. "Her choice is what matters. And she's chosen to stay here. With me."

Marcus's expression darkens. "An omega doesn't get choices. That's not how our world works, Sheriff. They need guidance. Control."

"Your world, maybe." Jake takes a step forward. "Not mine."

The tension thickens, both men's postures shifting subtly. This is no longer just a confrontation between sheriff and outsider. It's Alpha versus Alpha, two dominant wolves circling for position.

"I'm giving you one last opportunity to do this the civilized way," Marcus says. "Hand over Olivia and the child, and we'll leave peacefully. Refuse, and I'll be forced to challenge you formally. Winner takes all."

A formal challenge. The most primitive form of pack dispute resolution. Trial by combat.

My blood runs cold. Jake is strong, but Marcus is vicious. I've seen what he's capable of.

Before Jake can answer, movement catches my eye. Cars are pulling up along the road—locals from town. Marge from the diner. The teacher from Emma's school. Customers I've served coffee. They form a loose semicircle behind Jake's deputies, a silent wall of support.

One man steps forward—older, gray-haired, with an air of quiet authority. "This is Sanctuary Pack territory, stranger. Our Alpha's decision is final."

Marcus eyes the growing crowd with calculation. "Stay out of this, old man. Pack law allows for challenge when mates are disputed."

"Only legitimate matings," the older man counters. "And only with the omega's consent."

Jake looks at the newcomers, something like pride crossing his face. "Ellis is right. Sanctuary Pack doesn't recognize your claim."

Marcus's face contorts with rage. "You backward hicks think you can rewrite pack law? Challenge accepted!"

He shrugs off his jacket, tossing it to one of his men. Jake doesn't move.

"I haven't offered challenge," Jake says calmly. "You have no standing here."

"Then I'm taking her by force." Marcus signals to his men, who move forward as one.

"Stop!" The command bursts from me before I can think. I step onto the porch, ignoring Jake's warning look. "This is about me. I should have a say."

All eyes turn to me. Marcus's expression shifts to something almost tender—the mask he wore when we first met, before I knew the monster beneath.

"Livie, come home," he says, softening his voice. "I've forgiven your... indiscretion. We can be a family again."

"We were never a family," I say, finding strength in the truth. "You were my jailer, not my mate. And Emma deserves better than to grow up thinking that's what love looks like."

His false tenderness vanishes. "You ungrateful bitch. After everything I gave you—"

"I accept your challenge," Jake interrupts, stepping forward. "But let's be clear about the stakes. When I win, you leave. Permanently. No more contact. No more pursuit. Olivia and Emma are under Sanctuary Pack protection."

"And when I win," Marcus snarls, "she comes with me. Along with the brat."

"Over my dead body," Jake says simply.

The older man—Ellis—steps between them. "As Pack Elder, I'll officiate. Traditional rules. First to submit or become incapacitated loses. No weapons. No assistance."

I want to scream, to stop this primitive display, but I understand pack politics enough to know this is the cleanest resolution. If Jake wins through official challenge, Marcus loses all claim—not just legally, but in the eyes of any pack that respects tradition.

The two alphas move to a clear space in the yard, circling slowly. Jake removes his badge and gun, handing them to a deputy. Marcus rolls his shoulders, a confident smirk playing on his lips.

"Been a while since I put down an upstart Alpha," he taunts. "This will be fun."

Jake says nothing, his focus absolute. I've never seen this side of him—the pure Alpha, stripped of civilization's niceties. His movements are economical, predatory. Waiting.

Marcus strikes first, a lightning-fast blow that Jake barely dodges. They exchange a flurry of hits, testing defenses, looking for weaknesses. Marcus lands a solid punch to Jake's jaw that rocks him back. Blood appears at the corner of Jake's mouth.

My hands clench the porch railing so hard my knuckles turn white. Jake recovers quickly, blocking Marcus's next attack and countering with a vicious uppercut that snaps Marcus's head back.

The fight turns brutal. Both men bleeding, grunting with effort, neither willing to submit. Marcus fights dirty—a knee to the groin that Jake partially blocks, an attempt to gouge eyes that Jake twists away from. But Jake fights smart—conserving energy, making each blow count.

I see the moment the tide turns. Marcus overextends on a punch, and Jake slips inside his guard, delivering a devastating combination to ribs and solar plexus. Marcus staggers, gasping for breath. Jake presses the advantage, driving him back with relentless precision.

A sweeping kick takes Marcus's legs from under him. He hits the ground hard, Jake immediately on him, pinning him with a knee to the chest and an arm across his throat.

"Submit," Jake growls, increasing pressure.

Marcus struggles, face purpling, but he's beaten and knows it. "I... submit," he chokes out.

Jake holds him a moment longer, then rises, stepping back. Marcus rolls to his side, coughing and spitting blood.

"It's over," Ellis announces formally. "By right of challenge, Sheriff Hawkins has defended his claim. Sanctuary Pack recognizes his protection of Olivia Reed and her daughter. The challenger and his pack are banished from our territory."

Marcus's men shift uncomfortably, looking to their Alpha for direction. Slowly, painfully, Marcus pushes himself to his feet.

"This isn't over," he snarls, but the threat sounds hollow now.

"Yes, it is." Jake's voice carries the weight of absolute authority. "Ellis, as Pack Elder, witness my decree: Marcus Wilson and his associates are permanently banished from Sanctuary and all allied territories. Violation means immediate execution under pack law."

Ellis nods solemnly. "Witnessed and recorded."

Marcus's face twists with hatred, but even he recognizes the binding nature of pack decree. To violate it would make him an outlaw among all traditional packs—a death sentence in wolf society.

"You've made a mistake," he spits at me. "He'll tire of you eventually. They always do."

"Get out," I say simply. "And never come near my daughter again."

Something in my voice—perhaps the absolute certainty—finally penetrates. Marcus backs away, his men closing ranks around him, helping him to his car. The convoy leaves in sullen silence, dust billowing behind them.

Jake turns to me, bruised and bloodied but victorious. The crowd erupts in cheers and congratulations, but his eyes seek only mine.

I fly down the porch steps and into his arms, not caring who watches. He holds me tightly, his heartbeat strong against my cheek.

"Is it really over?" I whisper against his chest.

His arms tighten. "Yes. Pack decree is binding. He won't risk becoming an outlaw."

I pull back to examine his injuries—split lip, bruised jaw, knuckles raw and bleeding. "You're hurt."

"Worth it." His smile is fierce and tender all at once.

Looking around at the townspeople—my neighbors now, my pack—I feel something I haven't felt in years. Belonging. Safety. Home.

"Thank you," I say, not just to Jake but to all of them. "For fighting for us. For accepting us."

"You're one of us now," Marge calls out. "Pack protects its own."

One of us. Pack. Family. The words sink into my soul, healing places I thought permanently broken.

As Jake leads me back to the house, to Emma waiting inside, I realize Marcus was wrong about one thing. I'm not above my station. I've finally found exactly where I belong.

10

Night falls differently when you're not afraid. The shadows lack teeth, the silence feels like a blanket rather than a void. Emma sleeps soundly down the hall, exhausted from the day's drama but secure in the knowledge that the "bad man" is gone for good. Jake's house—our house now, I suppose—settles around us with comfortable creaks and sighs. I stand at the bedroom window, watching moonlight silver the trees, and feel the weight of two years on the run finally lifting from my shoulders. Free. We're truly free. The realization bubbles up from somewhere deep inside, threatening to overflow as a laugh or a sob, I'm not sure which.

"You okay?" Jake's voice comes soft from the doorway. He's showered, his injuries from the fight cleaned and bandaged. A bruise darkens his jaw, his split lip slightly swollen, but his eyes are clear and warm as they find mine.

"Better than okay." I turn from the window. "Just... processing."

He enters the room slowly, giving me space to retreat if I need it. Always so careful with my boundaries. "It's a lot to take in. Your whole life changed today."

"Our lives," I correct gently. "You fought for us. Claimed us publicly."

"I'd do it again." No hesitation, no doubt. "A hundred times over."

The certainty in his voice makes something warm unfurl in my chest. I move toward him, drawn by an invisible thread that's been there since the moment we met.

"Your face hurts," I say, reaching up to trace the edge of the bruise on his jaw.

He catches my hand, pressing a kiss to my palm. "Worth it."

"So you keep saying." My voice sounds breathless even to my own ears.

"Because it's true." His thumb traces circles on my wrist, over my pulse point. "You and Emma are worth everything."

The simple declaration undoes me. After years of being treated as property, as something to be possessed and controlled, Jake's steady respect feels like a revelation.

"I want to be your mate," I whisper. "Your true mate."

His eyes darken, pupils dilating. "Olivia—"

"Not because I feel obligated. Not because you fought for me today." I need him to understand this is my choice, freely made. "Because I love you. Because I trust you with myself and with Emma."

He draws a shaky breath. "Are you sure? After everything with Marcus—"

"That wasn't mating," I interrupt. "That was imprisonment. This—us—is real. What true mates should be."

Jake's control visibly frays, his scent sharpening with desire and something deeper—reverence. "I won't mark you unless you're absolutely certain. Once done—"

"I know. Permanent." I step closer, tilting my head to expose my neck, my scent glands. "That's what I want. You. Forever."

A tremor runs through him. His hand cups my cheek, tilting my face up. "I love you, Olivia. More than I thought possible."

"Show me," I whisper.

His mouth finds mine, gentle at first, mindful of his split lip. But gentleness quickly gives way to hunger. The kiss deepens, his tongue sweeping into my mouth, claiming, tasting. I press against him, arms winding around his neck, my body recognizing its mate and responding with immediate, overwhelming desire.

Jake lifts me effortlessly, my legs wrapping around his waist as he carries me to the bed. We fall together onto the mattress, hands exploring, tugging at clothing.

"Olivia," he groans, the sound vibrating under my mouth.

He helps me out of my shirt, eyes darkening further at the sight of me in just a simple cotton bra. Not sexy, not designed to entice, but the hunger in his gaze makes me feel beautiful anyway.

"Perfect," he murmurs, hands skimming up my sides. "So perfect for me."

His mouth trails sparks, slow and reverent, along the slope of my shoulder. He moves lower, pausing to nuzzle where my throat meets my collarbone, then lower still—lips dragging soft heat down to the edge of my bra. For a moment he just breathes me in, his hands splayed wide on my back, like he's trying to memorize the feeling of me. Then he palms the fabric, thumbs teasing the swell of my breasts until I can't help the desperate sound that escapes my lips.

He doesn't tease. He doesn't play by denying what we both want. Instead, he hooks a finger under the strap, pulls it down, exposes me inch by inch as if each millimeter is a holy revelation. When his mouth closes over my nipple, it isn't gentle; it's hungry. He sucks, teeth scraping, tongue licking circles that make my hips buck up into his. His hands roam, charting my ribs, my waist, the dip of my spine. It feels like I'm being claimed in a hundred tiny ways, each one leaving a mark deeper than any bruise.

I want to be marked. I want to be his.

I tug at his t-shirt, and he sits up enough for me to strip it off. There's a fresh bruise blooming under his pectoral, another along the line of his ribs. I run my fingers over them, feeling the tremor that ripples under his skin, and then, unable to resist, I press my lips to the darkest spot. He groans, a ragged, wounded sound, and the reverberation of it in my chest makes me shiver.

"Does it hurt?" I ask, not because I want him to stop, but because the caring is reflex now. Jake shakes his head, laughing breathless against my shoulder.

"I don't feel a thing except you," he says, so sincere it borders on sacred.

He turns his attention back to me, and in a blur my bra is gone. He worships every inch of newly revealed skin with mouth and hands, alternating between feather-light touches and deep, consuming kisses that leave me panting. I yank at his belt, desperate to feel all of him, but my hands are shaking. Jake slows me, taking over with steady competence. He undoes the button, slides the zipper down, peels away his jeans and briefs in one practiced move.

I can't stop staring. His body is built for violence, sure, but close up, there's a gentleness in the way he moves, the care he takes. His cock is thick and flushed and intimidating, but the way he looks at me—like I'm the only thing in the world that matters—makes the nerves dissolve into pure, heady want.

He kneels between my legs, hands pushing my knees apart, and for a moment just looks at me. No, more than looks—he studies, he admires. I feel bared to the bone, but never more treasured.

"You want this?" he asks, like consent is a sacred rite, not a formality.

I nod, too overcome to speak. Then he leans in and kisses the inside of my thigh, slow and unhurried, and everything inside me goes molten.

I reciprocate, wanting to learn him the same way he's learning me. I wrap my hand around his cock, marvel at the satin-soft skin stretched over rigid heat, the way the pulse pounds at the tip. He bites his lip when I stroke him, eyes fluttering closed, hips stuttering forward. I feel powerful and adored at once.

We undress the rest of the way in a tangle of limbs and laughter, awkward and sweet, until we're both bare and breathless and trembling. I lie back, and he covers me, the length of his body pressing me into the mattress.

He pauses, bracing himself above me, and for a beat we just look at each other—two people who have lost so much and dared to hope for more. His hair falls into his eyes. I brush it aside, fingers lingering on the sharp line of his cheekbone.

He shudders, but he doesn't rush. His hands cradle my face, his lips gentle on mine. When he finally lines himself up, he moves with agonizing slowness, giving me time to adjust, to want. The stretch is exquisite, almost too much, but I want all of it—all of him. He groans, face buried in my neck, and I feel his control slipping, barely held in check.

He withdraws just enough to look me in the eye. His voice is a near-growl.

"Last chance to change your mind," he says, voice strained with the effort of restraint.

In answer, I pull him down to me, our bodies aligning perfectly. The hard length of him presses against my core, already slick with desire. I roll my hips, drawing a growl from deep in his chest.

"Mine," he whispers against my throat, teeth grazing the sensitive skin there.

"Yours," I agree, spreading my thighs wider in invitation. "All of me."

He enters me slowly, giving me time to adjust to his size. The stretch is exquisite, familiar from our encounter in the shed but somehow more profound now. This isn't just sex—it's a claiming, a joining on every level. When he's fully seated inside me, he stills, our foreheads pressed together, sharing breath.

"I feel it," I whisper, amazed. "The bond."

"It's always been there," he says, voice rough with emotion. "Since the first moment."

He begins to move, setting a rhythm that builds steadily from gentle to urgent. I match him thrust for thrust, my body responding to his with instinctive knowledge. His scent envelops me—pine and musk and alpha strength, now tinged with the unmistakable notes of rut. My omega responds, my scent glands swelling with readiness.

Jake's movements grow more intense, more primal. His eyes glow alpha-gold in the dim light, fixed on my neck where my pulse hammers under thin skin. I tilt my head further, offering what we both need.

"Please," I gasp as pleasure builds to an almost unbearable peak. "Make me yours."

His rhythm falters, then steadies. One hand slides beneath me, lifting my hips to change the angle, hitting a spot inside that makes stars explode behind my eyelids. I feel his knot beginning to swell, pressing against my entrance with each thrust.

"Olivia," he groans, the sound almost pained. "I need—"

"Yes," I cut him off, wrapping my legs tighter around him. "Everything. All of you."

As his knot pushes inside me, stretching me to the edge of pain, his teeth find my scent gland. The dual sensation—being claimed, being filled—sends me over the edge. I shatter around him with a cry, pleasure radiating from every point of connection between us. As my inner walls clench around his knot, Jake bites down fully, breaking skin, sealing our bond.

The mating bite triggers his release. He pulses inside me, his knot locking us together as the bond snaps into place between us—a golden thread of connection I can feel almost physically. Emotions that aren't mine flood through me—Jake's fierce protectiveness, his wonder, his love. It's overwhelming, beautiful, terrifying in its intimacy.

We lie locked together, trembling with the aftershocks of pleasure and the newness of the bond. Jake licks gently at the bite mark, soothing the sting, his saliva sealing his claim. The gesture is primal but tender, making me shiver with renewed desire.

"I can feel you," he murmurs with wonder, propping himself on his elbows to look down at me. "In my head, in my chest. Everywhere."

"Me too." I touch his face, tracing the contours now familiar to my fingers. "It's like... coming home."

His smile is radiant. "That's exactly it. You're my home, Olivia. You and Emma."

"I never thought I'd have this," I confess, the safety of our connection making honesty easy.

"After Marcus, I didn't think I could trust anyone again, especially not an alpha."

"I'll spend the rest of my life earning that trust," he promises, shifting us carefully to our sides, still joined by his knot. "I'll never control you, never cage you. Your freedom is as important to me as your safety."

Tears sting my eyes at the simple vow—so different from the possessive claims Marcus made.

"I know," I whisper. "That's why I could choose this. Choose you."

Jake's hand comes to rest on my hip, his thumb tracing absent patterns on my skin. "I want to adopt Emma," he says suddenly. "Legally. Make her mine in the eyes of the law as well as the pack."

The unexpected declaration makes my heart swell. "You'd do that?"

"In a heartbeat. I already love her like she's my own. She's part of you, and that makes her part of me too."

I kiss him, pouring everything I can't yet put into words into the gesture. He responds with equal fervor, his hand sliding up to cup my breast, thumb circling the nipple until I gasp against his mouth.

"Again?" I ask, surprised as desire rekindles so quickly.

His smile turns wicked. "Mating night," he explains. "We'll be like this for hours. Maybe all night."

"Emma—"

"Is sound asleep and will stay that way until morning." He rolls his hips, his knot tugging slightly at my sensitive flesh. "We have time."

Time. Such a simple word, but it holds new meaning now. Time together. Time to build a life. Time to heal and grow and love without looking over our shoulders.

We make love again as his knot subsides, slower this time, savoring each touch, each kiss. The bond between us hums with shared pleasure, amplifying every sensation. When we finally fall asleep, tangled together, I feel safer than I have in years.

Morning brings sunlight streaming through curtains we forgot to close and the patter of small feet in the hallway. I barely have time to pull the sheet over our naked bodies before the door bursts open and Emma launches herself onto the bed.

"Mommy! Sheriff Daddy! Is the bad man really gone forever and ever?"

Jake catches her mid-bounce, tugging her down between us. His eyes meet mine over her head, a silent question. I nod, heart too full for words.

"Yes, squirt," he says, hugging her close. "He's gone forever. And it's just Daddy now, okay? No need for 'Sheriff' anymore."

11

One year. It's been one year since I stopped running, since I found the courage to stay and fight, since Jake claimed me as his mate. I stand on the back porch of our home—truly ours now, with the adoption papers making Jake officially Emma's father and the marriage certificate hanging framed in the hallway—watching my husband teach our daughter to shoot a bow. My hand rests on the swell of my belly, five months along with our second child. Jake Junior, he insists, though I'm equally convinced it's a girl. The future stretches before us, sunlit and secure in a way I once couldn't imagine. Sanctuary has lived up to its name.

"Elbow up, squirt," Jake instructs, adjusting Emma's stance. "That's it. Now draw back to your cheek. Steady."

Emma's face scrunches in concentration, tongue caught between her teeth. At six, she's all gangly limbs and determined spirit. The bow is child-sized but real—Jake believes in teaching actual skills, not watered-down versions.

"Now breathe out and release," he says softly.

The arrow flies, wobbling slightly but hitting the target—not the bullseye, but respectably close for her age. Emma squeals, jumping up and down.

"I did it, Daddy! I did it!"

"You sure did." Jake's face glows with pride as he high-fives her. "Pretty soon you'll be outshootin' me."

"And then I can help protect the baby," Emma announces, patting my belly as I join them. "Right, Mommy?"

"The baby is very lucky to have such a brave big sister," I agree, smoothing her wild curls.

Jake's arm slides around my waist, his hand joining mine on my stomach. His touch still sends warmth coursing through me, the mate bond humming contentedly between us. Through it, I feel his happiness, his pride, his unwavering love.

"How are you today?" he asks, kissing my temple.

"I'm good." I lean into him, savoring his strength. "Though your baby is practicing karate on my bladder."

Jake's smile widens. He drops to his knees, pressing his face to my belly. "Go easy on your mama, little man."

"Girl," I correct, tugging him back up.

"We'll see." His eyes crinkle at the corners. "Either way, perfect."

Emma tugs at his hand. "Can I shoot again? Please?"

"Three more arrows," he agrees. "Then we need to get ready for Mommy's party."

The baby shower. Marge insisted on throwing it at the diner, closing early for the private celebration. "For our pack's newest member," she'd said, as if there was never any question I belonged.

Later, surrounded by women from town—the deputy's wife who watched Emma during the confrontation with Marcus, Emma's kindergarten teacher, Marge and her niece, even the motel clerk who first checked us in—I find myself blinking back tears at their genuine excitement for our growing family.

"Open mine next," Marge says, pushing a large gift bag toward me.

Inside is a handmade quilt, each square contributed by a different woman in the room. Photos, baby clothes patterns, even tiny paw prints representing the pack.

"We all added something," Marge explains. "So the little one knows they've got a whole community watching out for them."

I run my fingers over the stitches, the care evident in every seam. "I don't know what to say."

"You don't need to say anything, honey." Marge pats my hand. "You're pack now. This is what we do."

Pack. Family. The words still hold wonder for me, even after a year.

The weekend brings warmer weather and our ritual family picnic at the lake. Jake grills burgers while Emma and I set up the blanket and unpack the cooler. This spot has become ours—a small clearing with a perfect view of the water, sheltered by pines.

"Race you to the dock!" Emma challenges, already sprinting ahead.

"Careful!" I call, though I know Jake is watching her like a hawk, his protective instincts only heightened since I became pregnant.

"She's fine," he assures me, flipping a burger. "I taught her to swim last summer, remember? She's practically a fish now."

I settle onto the blanket, watching Emma leap and twirl at the end of the dock, her joy infectious. "She's thriving here."

Jake sits beside me, one hand automatically finding mine, the other resting on my belly. "So are you."

"I am." The simple acknowledgment feels significant. "I never thought I'd have this, Jake. Safety. Happiness. A real family."

His kiss is gentle, reverent. "You deserve all of it and more."

That evening brings the Sanctuary Spring Festival—strings of lights in the town square, music, dancing, the community gathered in celebration. Different from the festival where Jake and I first gave in to our desire, but familiar in its warmth and inclusivity.

Jake, resplendent in his sheriff's uniform, takes the microphone to officially open the festivities. His eyes find me in the crowd, and his smile widens.

"Before we kick things off, I want to introduce the most important people in my life." He beckons us forward. "My mate, Olivia. Our daughter, Emma. And—" his hand touches my belly, "—little Jake Junior on the way."

"Or little Lily," I counter into the microphone, drawing laughter from the crowd.

"My family," Jake continues, his voice thick with emotion. "My heart."

As the music starts and the dancing begins, I watch Emma twirl with the other children, her face alight with uncomplicated joy. Jake pulls me close, swaying gently to accommodate my pregnant belly.

"Happy?" he murmurs against my hair.

"Complete," I correct, the word encompassing everything I feel.

Over his shoulder, I catch sight of Marge raising a glass in our direction. Ellis, the pack elder, nods in approval. The deputy's wife waves Emma into a children's dance circle. My people. My pack. My home.

Later, tucked into bed with Jake's warm body curled protectively around mine, his hand splayed possessively over our growing child, I reflect on the journey that brought us here. Two years ago, I was running for my life, convinced safety was just a temporary illusion. Now I understand that safety isn't about locks and hiding places. It's about belonging. About being surrounded by people who would fight for you, who see your value beyond your designation as omega or mother or mate.

"I can hear you thinking," Jake murmurs sleepily, pressing a kiss to my mating mark. The scar has faded to silver, but the bond it represents has only strengthened.

"Good thoughts," I assure him, snuggling closer. "Just grateful."

"Mmm." His hand makes slow, soothing circles on my belly. "Me too. Every day."

The baby kicks against his palm, and Jake's answering rumble of pleasure vibrates through my back. "See? Junior agrees."

"Lily," I insist with a smile.

"We'll see." His arms tighten around me. "Get some sleep, mate. I've got you."

And he does. In all the ways that matter, he has me, and I have him. We have each other, this family we've built, this life we've chosen.

As sleep claims me, I send a silent message to the desperate woman I was a year ago, running scared with a child in tow and no hope for the future: It gets better. You find home. You find pack. You find the mate who sees you—really sees you—and loves you not despite your broken places, but because of how beautifully you've pieced yourself back together.

In the morning, Emma will crawl into our bed, as she does every weekend, chattering about dreams and plans for the day. Jake will make pancakes, his specialty. Life will continue, ordinary and extraordinary in its simple security.

And I will wake each day in this sanctuary we've built—not just the town, but the space between us, the family we've formed—and know that I am finally, truly home.

Find out what happens next in Sanctuary with Colt and Sunny's story in The Alpha Mechanic! (https://readerlinks.com/l/5019889)

(Continue to the next page for a Bonus Epilogue.)

Want more of Jake and Olivia? Sign up for my newsletter and download a free bonus scene today! The Alpha Sheriff Bonus Scene (https://www.ashjadeauthor.com/alphasheriffbo nus)

BONUS EPILOGUE

SUNNY

The road stretches ahead, winding through mountains painted gold and purple by the dying sun. Beautiful. Haunting. Empty. Just the way I need it to be—no scents but pine and exhaust, no eyes watching my every move. I force a laugh that sounds hollow even to my own ears. Who am I kidding?

I pull over at the overlook, gravel spitting under the tires, and let the engine idle while I step out to stretch my legs. The sudden silence slams into me—no local radio, no navigation voice, no humming AC—just the thin, predatory whine of wind at altitude and the metal tick tick tick of the cooling hood. The mountain air hits sharp and clean, a blade of cold that cuts straight through my hoodie and the ratty T-shirt I've been living in for two days. I hug myself, but the shiver isn't just from the chill.

The view is ridiculous, like some battered old postcard left in a gas station rack for a decade too long. Below, valleys fold and refold into infinite origami shadows, seams crisp and bottomless, the green gone black in the dusk. Peaks catch the last stubborn rays of sunlight and hold them captive, fiery gold bruising into purple at the tips. There are no cars behind me, no evidence that civilization ever breached this far but for the crumbling guardrail and a scattering of beer bottles by the faded trail marker. Even the birds are silent—too late in the season, or maybe they're just smart enough to bed down before the real predators wake up.

I lean against the hood, hoping the residual warmth might convince my body to relax, but my muscles stay coiled and jittery. My hands won't unclench, fists jammed into my pockets, worrying the seams until the thread bites into my skin. I try focusing on the little things: the coyote yelp echoing somewhere off to the left, the clean snap of windblown branches, the resin tang of pine needles crushed underfoot. All it does is remind me how far I am from anywhere that matters.

For a second, I let myself imagine—just for a heartbeat—that I could keep driving, keep running, and the world would simply blur behind me until nothing left could catch up. That I could become one of those stories, a name on a missing poster no one ever finds, a ghost haunting every highway diner and truck stop west of the Mississippi. I let that version of me breathe, inhale the freedom, the terror, the ache of it. Is this what relief feels like? Or just another flavor of panic, seasoned with too much altitude and not enough oxygen?

I wipe my eyes with the back of my hand, pretending it's just from the wind. No one to see. No one to mind.

"You're fine," I tell myself, the words snatched away the moment they leave my lips. "Just fine."

My car disagrees, metal ticking as it cools, a suspicious puddle forming underneath. I kick the front tire, instantly regretting it when pain stabs through my sneaker.

"Damn it, Sunny, real smart."

That's when I see it—a weathered road sign, half-hidden by overgrown brush. I walk closer, brushing aside brambles to read the faded letters: SANCTUARY, 15 MILES.

Back in the driver's seat, I twist the key. The engine turns over, then catches with a wet, hacking sound that makes my stomach drop. The dashboard lights flicker like dying fireflies.

"Come on, Betsy, just a little further." I pat the cracked vinyl dashboard. "We've still got places to be."

Places that aren't home. No, not home. That's not what I left.

I ease back onto the road, wincing at every ping and rattle. My phone sits dark and silent in the cup holder—battery dead, contacts purged before I left. Better that way. Can't call for help, but can't be tracked either.

"Sanctuary," I say aloud, testing the word on my tongue. It sounds too good to be true. Places don't offer sanctuary anymore, not for omegas like me. Every town has its pecking order, its territorial alphas, its rules written in pheromones and pack politics.

Still, the name tugs at something in me. Fifteen miles. I could walk it by morning if I had to.

The landscape changes subtly. The wilderness feels less wild somehow, more watched. I pass a wooden fence line, weathered but maintained. Then a mailbox. Then a small homestead set back from the road, lights glowing warm in the windows.

Signs of life. Signs of civilization. My shoulders ease a fraction.

The road begins to descend, curving through a forested valley. Through gaps in the trees, I catch glimpses of a small town nestled below—streetlights coming on one by one, buildings clustered along what looks like a main street.

Sanctuary.

Find out what happens next with Colt and Sunny in The Alpha Mechanic! (https://readerlinks.com/l/5019889)

<u>The Sanctuary Pack Series</u>

Welcome to Sanctuary.
A hidden mountain town where omegas come to heal—and alphas learn what it means to protect.

About Ash Jade

Ash Jade writes trope-packed omegaverse romances full of heat, ruts, and fated mates — but always with heart. Her stories are fast, messy, and addictive, blending primal passion with emotional cores that make the bonds hit even harder. If you love bingeable romances where instinct tangles with feelings (and always ends in happily-ever-after), you've found your pack.

ashjadeauthor.com